First published in Great Britain 2024 by Farshore
An imprint of HarperCollins*Publishers*,
1 London Bridge Street, London SE1 9GF
www.farshore.co.uk

HarperCollins*Publishers*
Macken House, 39/40 Mayor Street Upper, Dublin 1, D01 C9W8, Ireland

Written by Laura Jackson.

© 2024 Disney Enterprises, Inc.

ISBN 978 0 00 871157 3
Printed and bound in Romania
001

A CIP catalogue record for this title is available from the British Library.

Parental guidance is advised for all craft and colouring activities. Always ask an adult to help when using glue, paint and scissors. Wear protective clothing and cover surfaces to avoid staining.

Stay safe online. Farshore is not responsible for content hosted by third parties.

This Disney M@ANA Annual 2025 belongs to

....

....

Age ....

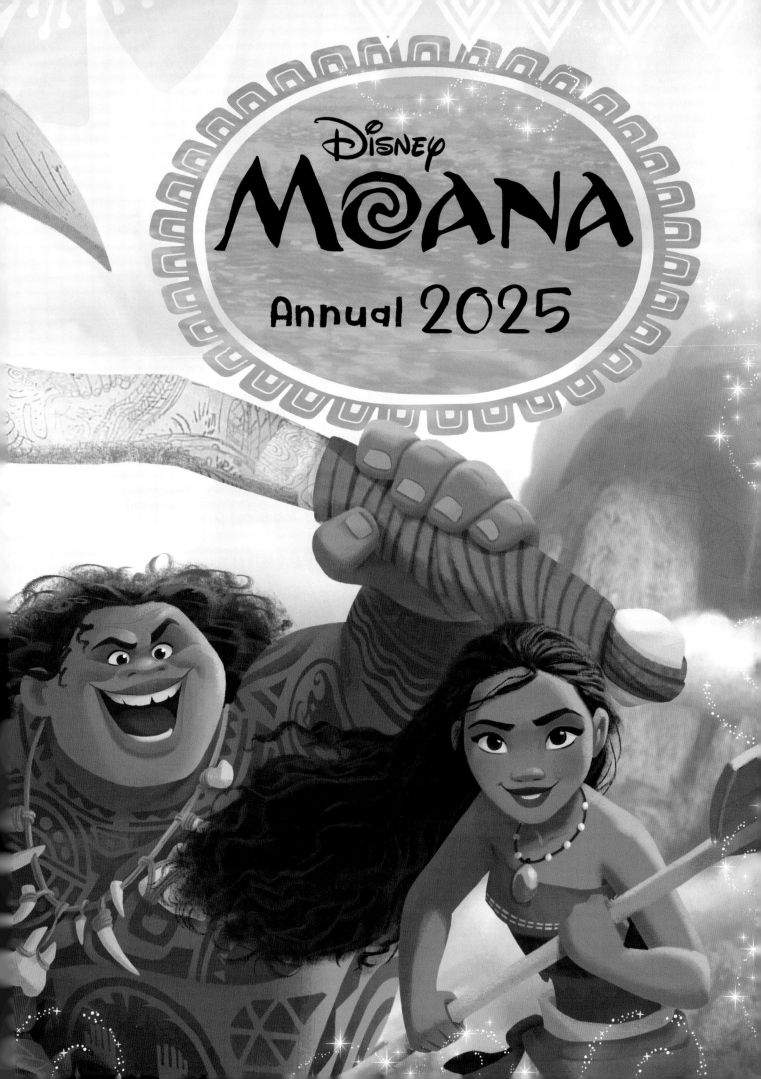

Contents

Meet Moana

Moana is a brave leader who has dreamed of exploring **the ocean** ever since she was a baby. Even when her father, Chief Tala, told her to **not sail** beyond the reef, she was determined to be a **true ocean voyager!**

Moana has always loved exploring, swimming and surfing in the ocean.

Moana's best friend is her pet pig, Pua.

Moana dreams of becoming an expert wayfinder, just like her ancestors.

Spirit of the Ocean

When the ocean calls, Moana listens. Help little Moana race to the ocean to start her adventure.

START

Don't bump into Chief Tala. He wants Moana to stay on dry land today!

FINISH

Answer on page 69.

Welcome to Motunui

Motunui is an island full of palm trees, flowers, waterfalls, wildlife and beautiful beaches. Follow the path through the island and meet Moana's family and friends along the way.

START →

Sima is Moana's smart, nature-loving mother. While she supports her daughter's wish to explore beyond the reef, she will do everything she can to protect her.

Chief Tala is Moana's father and the leader of Motunui. Like Moana, he can be stubborn and determined, but his love for his family and his people shows he has a soft side too!

Gramma Tala's spirit lives on in the ocean and in Moana's memories. She was a wonderful storyteller, and now Moana loves telling her own stories – just like her Gramma.

Can you spot this **turtle** on Motunui?

Pua is Moana's loyal, lovable pet pig. He brings all his bouncy energy to every fun adventure.

Heihei is the village rooster. He is always in the wrong place at the wrong time and causes lots of chaos. But Moana is sure he has an inner strength just waiting to be revealed!

How many **pink flowers** can you count?

→ FINISH

Life is Back!

Follow the story all about Moana's brave mission to save Motunui. When you get to a picture, say the word out loud.

 Moana   flowers   fish   fruit   ocean   Te Fiti   stars

When her island home of Motunui was in danger,

 knew she had to save her land and her family.

All the had stopped growing, had

disappeared from the and all the

had dried up. As a darkness threatened to take

over, Moana bravely set off across the to find

the source of nature on Motunui – the goddess .

After travelling far beyond the reef using

the , wind and currents to guide her,

discovered that the heart of itself was

missing! The heart was a precious stone that helped

 create life and nature. had to find

it to save her people!

 bravely battled mighty foes to take the stone

back. When she returned the precious heart back to

 , nature was soon restored again on Motunui.

Now, the island is blooming with , the

is full of beautiful 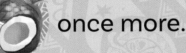 and the trees are bursting

with 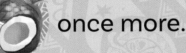 once more.

 saved her home! And she is ready to share

her skills with a whole new generation of wayfarers.

It's time for a new voyage ...

Meet Maui

Maui is a **demigod** – half mortal, half god, all awesome! He might be the ultimate **trickster** and a big show-off, but underneath it all he just wants to be a brave **hero**.

Maui is super strong and loves to muscle up!

Maui's magical hook gives him the power to shapeshift into any animal.

Maui is a wayfinder and teaches Moana everything he knows.

Maui's Tattoos

Maui's tattoos have special meanings. Each marking is a reminder of big things that have happened in his life.

Put a tick (✔) next to the tattoo close-ups you can spot in this picture. Add a cross (✗) to the trick tattoos that don't belong.

a ☐　b ☐　c ☐　d ☐　e ☐　f ☐

Make Your Mark

Design a symbol that represents something important from your life.

Answers on page 69.

Journey to Friendship

When Moana and the demigod Maui met for the first time, it seemed very unlikely they'd become good friends. But on their journey to restore the heart of Te Fiti and save their world, they learned to support each other to face all the dangers they met along their way, and their bond grew stronger. Relive some of the most exciting moments that led to Moana and Maui's special friendship ...

1

Since she was really young, Moana had listened to Maui's story and she was really curious about his adventures on the ocean. She also loved boats and being close to the sea, just like the wayfinding demigod.

2

When Moana decided to set sail and try to restore the heart of Te Fiti, she shipwrecked on Maui's island and met the demigod face to face. At first, they didn't get along!

3

Maui tried to leave Moana behind, but her determination was powerful! Thanks to the ocean's help, she reached Maui on the boat and promised to help him retrieve his magical fishhook, if he followed her on her mission!

4

Their journey didn't start in the best way, but they soon learned to stick together and support each other. After fighting the Kakamora, they reached Lalotai and retrieved Maui's magical fishhook from the terrible Tamatoa!

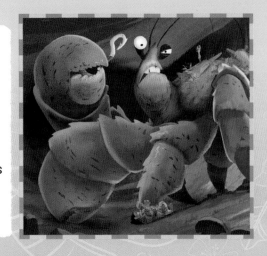

5

Soon they realised that, after all, they could try to be friends. Maui taught Moana about the secrets of wayfinding, and she helped him realise that he could be strong and great, even without his fishhook!

6

When they sailed beyond the barrier and confronted Te Kā, they unfortunately had to retreat because the monster was too powerful and cracked Maui's fishhook!

7

Maui was so discouraged that he left Moana alone. But when Moana decided to fight against Te Kā again, Maui came back. He transformed into a hawk and helped her confront the monster and discover the truth about Te Fiti.

8

When the two heroes finally restored the heart of Te Fiti, they realised that their relationship had grown into a strong friendship. Together, they saved their world and they will never forget about their awesome adventures!

Your World

Friends, family (and pets!) make Moana's life full of fun, love and adventure. Draw some of the special people and animals in your world below.

Tell Moana your favourite thing about each person or animal!

Sisters

Forever

Disney
M@ANA 2

Fear the Kakamora

The Kakamora are on the attack! Grab a pencil and guide Heihei to Moana's boat. If your pencil touches the sides, run back and start again.

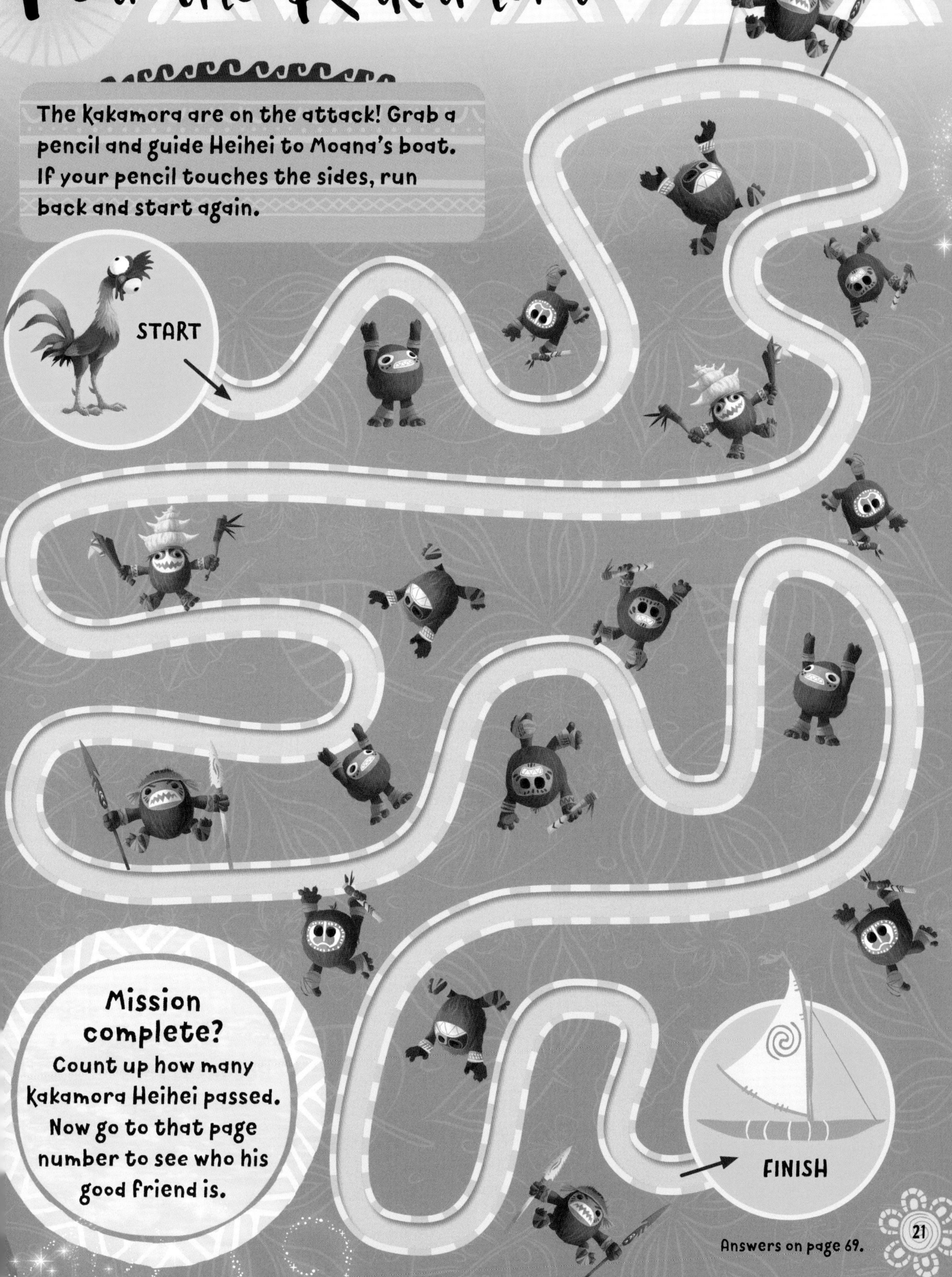

START

Mission complete?
Count up how many Kakamora Heihei passed. Now go to that page number to see who his good friend is.

FINISH

Answers on page 69.

Joking Around

Maui might seem scary sometimes, but he loves to make people laugh. Rate the ultimate trickster's jokes out of 10.

What did the ocean do when it saw Moana?

It waved!

10

Why did the shark blush?

Because the seaweed!

10

What does a dolphin say when he's confused?

Can you be more Pacific?

10

Why did Tamatoa want to keep all the treasure for himself?

Because he is shell-fish!

10

Now tell Maui your favourite joke!

Why is the ocean so strong?

Because it has lots of mussels!

10

22

Flower Power

Te Fiti is the goddess of nature, and she needs your help to nurture these flowers back to life. Colour the blooms with your brightest pencils.

You could use this flower key to help you choose colours.

 orange

 pink

 red

 yellow

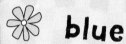 blue

23

A New Voyage

When Moana hears the call of her ancestors, she knows she must travel further than she has ever gone before. Help Moana navigate across the darkest ocean to Maui. It's time they face a new mission, together.

START →

Answer on page 69.

Stay away from the whirlpool!

TIP:
the ancestor's ships will help guide the way!

FINISH

25

A Sign in the Stars

Gramma Tala always told Moana to look to the stars to guide her. Join up the stars to reveal three pictures hidden in the sky.

1 (dot-to-dot: 1, 2, 3, 4, 5, 6, 7, 8, 9, 10, 11, 12, 13, 14, 15, 16, 17, 18, 19, 20)

2 (dot-to-dot: 1, 2, 3, 4, 5, 6, 7, 8, 9, 10, 11, 12, 13, 14, 15, 16, 17, 18, 19, 20)

3 (dot-to-dot: 1, 2, 3, 4, 5, 6, 7, 8, 9, 10, 11, 12, 13, 14, 15, 16, 17, 18, 19, 20)

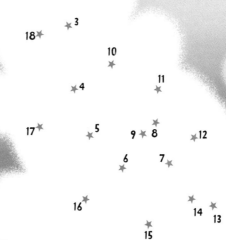

Now use the clues to fill in the missing words to help Moana work out her mission.

1 Journey far across the **w** _ _ _ _ .

2 Find Maui and his magical **h** _ _ _ _ .

3 Look for a **b** _ _ _ _ to set sail in!

Answers on page 69.

Nature's Treasures

The Island of Motunui is bursting and blooming with treasures from nature. Count up the different groups of items Moana and Pua spotted on their walk today.

a How many bunches of bananas?

bunches of bananas

b How many pieces of sugar cane in the baskets?

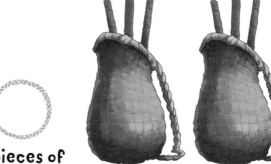

pieces of sugar cane

c How many shells at the beach?

shells

d How many purple flowers?

purple flowers

Answers on page 69.

1 Which group has the **highest** number?

2 Which group has the **lowest** number?

Set Sail

Moana is getting ready for a new mission across the ocean. Colour the picture and learn all about the boat before she sets sail.

The **sail** uses wind to move the boat forwards.

The **spiral** is a symbol of hope and new beginnings.

Moana uses her **oar** to speed up, turn around and stop.

The **ropes** are made of coconut fibre.

Adventure Starts Here

Imagine you are travelling across the ocean with Moana in her boat. Fill in this travel log as you go.

The weather is:

sunny   rainy   lightning

windy   cloudy

Tick (✔) your choice.

Who is travelling with you?

1 ....
2 ....
3 ....

The best thing about today:

....

....

....

I ate:

....

....

....

....

How I felt today. Colour in your choice.

We discovered ...

Now colour in your Moana badge.

I voyaged with **Moana**

A Pig Named Pua

One day, Chief Tala carried a pig and her baby piglets onto the beach. He was taking them to live with a farmer on the other side of the island.

"Why don't you come with me?" he asked Moana. "We can take the boat, it's faster."

Moana ran straight out to the boat. There was nothing better than being out on the ocean!

She kept the pigs safe as Chief Tala steered across the waves.

"The smallest piglet isn't getting any food," Moana noticed.

But there was no time to tend to the piglets, the waves were getting stronger.

Moana helped her father as the waves ripped and roared.

"It looks like the ocean goes on forever!" Moana gasped.

"It is dangerous," warned Chief Tala. "That's why we don't go beyond the reef..."

When the shore was in sight, Chief Tala steered the boat back to land. Moana couldn't help but notice the smallest piglet again. It still wasn't getting any food.

"Help me pull the boat in!" said Chief Tala. "Then you can worry about the piglet!"

As she helped Tala pull the boat ashore, Moana kept glancing back at the little piglet.

Moana and Chief Tala safely brought the pigs to the farmer's pen, but the mother pig still seemed too busy with the bigger piglets to have time for the littlest one.

"They're not giving him a chance!" said Moana.

"Sometimes that happens with a big litter," said the farmer.

Moana couldn't bear the thought of the little piglet being left out. She gently picked him out of his pen.

"Maybe I can feed you," she whispered.

She acted quickly and rolled up a leaf and filled it with coconut milk. The little piglet drank until he was full and happy!

"You are Pua," said Moana.
In that moment, Moana and Pua each knew they had found a great friend.

"I fed him and he ate!" Moana told Tala and the farmer.

The farmer chuckled. "I think that means he's yours," he said.

Tala gave Moana a stern look but he didn't say she couldn't keep the piglet.

"His name is Pua!" Moana announced as she got back on the boat.

"Well, put Pua down and help us get home," smiled Tala. And she did. Moana dipped the sail and helped her father navigate the big ocean waves.

From that night on, Pua slept beside Moana. Whenever he woke, she fed him with coconut milk and he became bigger and stronger.

As Pua grew, so did their friendship. Pua brought Moana gifts, like little coconuts and seashells.

And they would play games and pretend they were fishing in the ocean.

At the end of each day, the friends would watch the sunset, enjoying the way the light danced on the ocean and more than anything else ... being together.

Ocean Fun

Out on the ocean is Moana's happy place.
Can you spot six differences between these two pictures?
Colour in a star each time you spot one.

Answers on page 69.

2

Where is your happy place? Draw it here!

Game On!

Maui and Moana are having a competition to see who is the best wayfinder today. Challenge a friend in a game of tic-tac-toe to find out who wins!

How to Play:

- Choose who is Maui and who is Moana.
- If you are Maui, draw a hook.
- If you are Moana, draw a star.
- Take it in turns to draw in the squares, the first to get to three in a row – across, down or diagonally, wins that game.

GAME 1

GAME 2

GAME 3

The best wayfinder today is:

....

Secret Shapeshifters

Maui can shapeshift into a whale, a pig, a beetle ... you name it! Colour in the picture using the dots as a colour guide to reveal the two animals he turned into today.

Answers on page 69.

Memories

Gramma Tala loves to tell tales of her ancestors. Study the picture for 10 seconds. Now cover it up and take the memory quiz.

1. Is it night or day?

2. What animal is on the sand?

3. Is Gramma Tala sitting down or standing up?

4. Who is Pua next to?

5. How many shells are on the beach?

Answers on page 69.

Best Friends

Moana and Pua love hanging out. Life is always fun when they are together. Draw hearts by the two pictures that match.

1

2

3

4

5

6

Answers on page 69.

A Day with Moana

It was a sunny day on Motunui. Moana was taking the village children on an adventure to collect sugar cane.

"We have to stick together," said Moana. "The island is big. If you get lost, stay where you are and I'll find you."

"We promise!" said the children, who were excited to spend a day with Moana.

The island was full of giant trees, colourful plants and boulders in all shapes and sizes.

"How can you tell where you're going?" the children asked Moana.

Moana always knew where she was on Motunui. She used the signs in nature to find her way.

"See, that rock over there looks a little like Pua ...

... and these vines look like Heihei!" Moana laughed. "I look for visual signs in nature and remember them."

As the sun burned brightly the air grew muggy and warm, so the group stopped for a break.

The children scrambled up trees to pick fresh coconuts and broke them open on the rocks. The sweet water inside cooled everyone down.

Tao, one of the boys from the group, had noticed a colourful bird he had never seen before.

"Maybe it blew in on a storm," he thought.

He was so interested in the little bird, he forgot all about staying close to Moana.

He followed the bird deeper and deeper into the island, all the way back to its nest.

Tao was proud of his discovery! But he suddenly realised he was far from the group and he didn't know how to get back.

Tao started to feel worried, but then he remembered Moana had told him to stay put if he got lost.

He just hoped his friends would find him soon!

Before long, Moana had noticed Tao was missing. She quickly gathered the children and they raced back past the vines that looked like Heihei and towards the Pua-shaped rock.

It was there that Moana noticed blue feathers blowing in the breeze.

"Maybe he went this way ..." Moana said, following the trail.

The feathers led them all the way to a clearing ... where there was somebody sitting on a rock.

"Tao!" the children cheered happily.

Tao was so happy to see Moana and his friends! He was even more excited to show them his bird discovery.

Moana looked up at the bird with its chicks. "Looks like everyone is back together now," she smiled.

Up in the sky, the sun was beginning to set. Moana led the children to the sugar cane field and they set to work. When their baskets and arms were full, they headed back to the village.

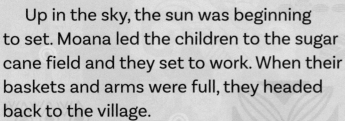

"Before we go, let's make a sign," said Moana.

They carved a drawing of the blue bird into the ground. Now they had a new sign to mark the way to the sugar cane field. It was the perfect way to end their day.

Soon, Moana and the children arrived back at the village, all ready for bed. Moana gave each child a hongi, by pressing her nose up against theirs.

"When I grow up, I want to be just like you!" said Tao.

Moana was touched. "As Gramma Tala used to say, 'you will be everything you want to be.'"

Moana's heart felt as full as her basket of sugar cane.

Race to Te Fiti

Moana needs to get to Te Fiti – and fast. But with the Kakamora and Te Kā trying to stop her, the challenge is on! Race against a friend to see who reaches Te Fiti first.

You will need:
- 2+ players
- A dice
- some counters (you could use coins, shells, stones or pieces of paper)

54 55 56
53 52 51
36 37 38
35 34 33
18 19 20
17 16 15
START 1

How to Play:

- Take turns to roll the dice.
- Move forward the same number of spaces rolled.
- The first player to reach Te Fiti is the winner!

If you land on Maui, ride **UP** the waves.

If you land on Gramma Tala, follow the trail **UP** to the manta ray.

If you land on Te Kā, shoot **DOWN** the lava flow.

If you land on the Kakamora, fall **DOWN** the coconuts.

57

58

59

60

FINISH

50

49

48

47

46

45

39

40

41

42

43

44

32

31

30

29

28

27

21

22

23

24

25

26

14

13

12

11

10

9

3

4

5

6

7

8

49

Under the Waves

There are so many amazing creatures in the sea. Come and explore the ocean with Moana and take the splashy quiz.

1 Draw what comes next ...

2 Circle the odd one out ...

a  b  c  d

3 Circle the manta ray's matching shadow.

 a  b 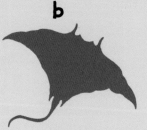 c

The **manta ray** is Gramma Tala's spirit animal. It symbolises strength and wisdom.

4 Circle the BIGGEST wave.

a  b   c  d  e

Answers on page 69.

Nature Hunt

Gramma Tala and Sima taught Moana to always respect and look after nature. Go outdoors and see how many amazing things you can see and hear in nature today.

I can see ...

cloud ☐

sun ☐

flower ☐

tree ☐

leaf ☐

stone ☐

plant ☐

water ☐

bird ☐

spider's web ☐

I can hear ...

1 ....

2 ....

3 ....

Don't forget to take a grown-up with you on your hunt!

Musical Puzzle

Dancing to drumbeats has always been a big, happy, noisy part of life on Motunui. Write the numbers of the missing pieces in the correct spaces below.

Answers on page 69.

Wayfinders

Maui has lost his magical hook and needs it back. Find a route through the ocean to Maui's hook by following the pictures in this order:

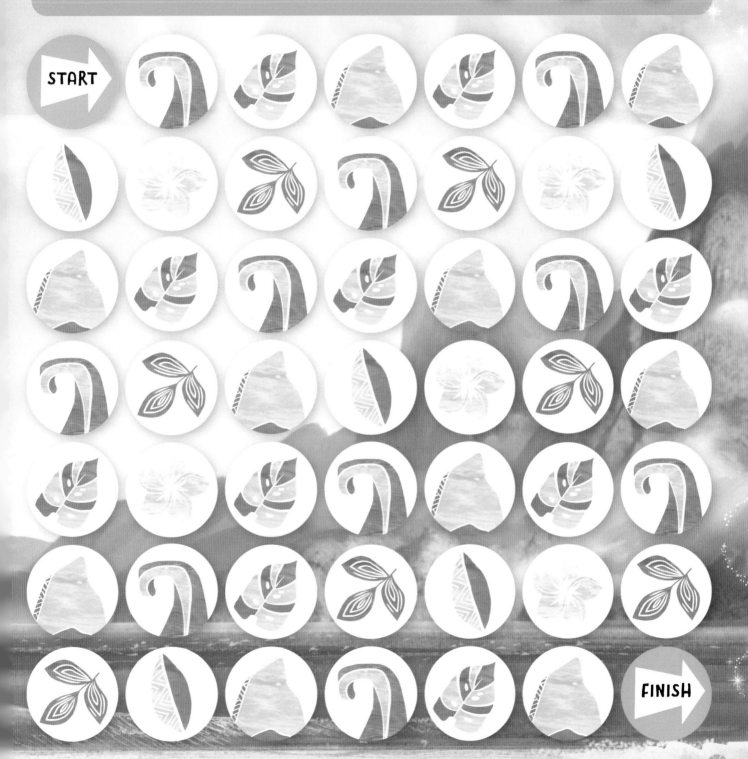

Answers on page 69.

Quiz Quest

Are you ready to be a wayfinding adventurer with Moana? Do you know your kakamora from your coconuts? Or Te kā from Tamatoa? Take the test to find out!

1 What do Moana and Maui use to guide them across the ocean?

a stars, currents and sun
b coconuts, flowers and shells
c sharks, fish and bubbles

2 Who is Te Fiti?

a a chicken
b the goddess of nature and life
c a crab

3 What symbol is on Moana's boat sail?

a a swirl
b a star
c a flower

4 What do the kakamora use as armour?

a oars
b coconut shells
c bananas

5 Who were Moana's ancestors?

a voyagers
b artists
c actors

6 What is this?

a Moana's oar
b the heart of Te Fiti
c Maui's magical hook

1 – 3

Stay on shore for a bit longer. You have lots of exciting things to learn!

7 What does Tamatoa like to steal?

a shiny things
b fruit
c pigs

8 Who told Moana that "the ocean chose you"?

a Heihei
b Pua
c Gramma Tala

4 – 6

You are ready to join Moana and Maui on the water, but don't go beyond the reef!

9 Te kā is the spirit of ...

a ice
b fire and volcanoes
c waves

7 – 9

You're an expert wayfinder! You can now set sail on an epic ocean adventure.

Answers on page 69.

Moana's Message

Moana has a special message – just for you! Crack the code to reveal her adventurous advice.

Answers on page 69.

Beach Clean-up

There has been a big storm in the night, things have blown all over the island – and on Pua and Heihei! Help Moana keep the beach clean by circling the items to tidy ...

Now count each item.

Answers on page 69.

Becoming Shiny

Moana was getting ready to tell the children in her village a story, just like Gramma Tala used to do.

"Tell us a scary story!" said one of the children.

Moana smiled and began a tale about the realm of monsters ...

"When Maui and I were on an adventure to find the heart of Te Fiti, we visited Lalotai and met a giant crab monster called Tamatoa! Tamatoa collected shiny things. He had stolen Maui's magical hook, so we needed to get to his lair to take it back."

"Wait!" a little boy cried out. "Why did Tamatoa like shiny things?"

"Well, he thought he could make himself beautiful by putting shiny things on his shell. He thought outer beauty was more important than inner beauty."

Moana continued her story.

"When Tamatoa was growing up, he wanted to hear stories about Maui! Maui defeated monsters and was known for his powerful hook and magical tattoos.

Tamatoa wanted to be feared by everyone too, including Maui. But to do that, he needed ... a look."

"He tried covering himself with kelp and sea urchins and rocks, but nothing quite worked, until he discovered a shiny necklace and placed it on his shell.

From then on, Tamatoa was hooked. He stole from men and monsters, making new enemies wherever he went.

Over the years, his collection grew and grew. He was often alone, but that didn't bother him.

'I'm the most glittery one in the room anyway!' he would say."

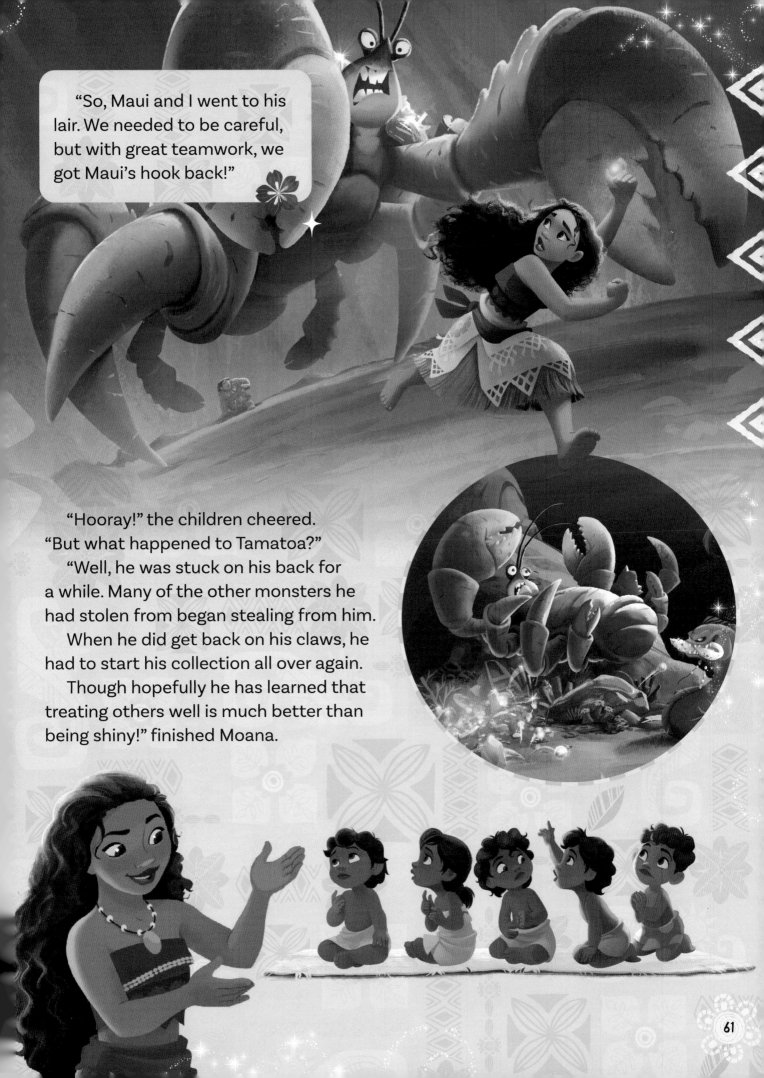

"So, Maui and I went to his lair. We needed to be careful, but with great teamwork, we got Maui's hook back!"

"Hooray!" the children cheered. "But what happened to Tamatoa?"

"Well, he was stuck on his back for a while. Many of the other monsters he had stolen from began stealing from him.

When he did get back on his claws, he had to start his collection all over again.

Though hopefully he has learned that treating others well is much better than being shiny!" finished Moana.

Something's Changed

Maui is up to his old tricks again, and has made changes to these pictures.
Cross the odd one out in each circle.

Answers on page 69.

Disney
M@ANA 2

Disney

MOANA 2

Best Friends!

Motivate Your Day

Gramma Tala always helped Moana find her truth and be the best she can be. Use these motivational cards to bring the power of positivity to your day!

© Disney

You are going to go far.

© Disney

Be who you are on the inside.

© Disney

You can be a hero.

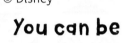
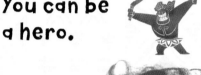

© Disney

Say 'yes' to an adventure!

© Disney

You bring fun to the world.

You are a good friend.

© Disney

Share your magic with the world.

How to Use Your Cards:

- Ask a grown-up to cut out the cards.
- Put them next to your bed.
- Each morning, pick a card to feel inspired and try new challenges.

Help someone out today.

Talk about what makes you proud to be YOU!

Write down three dreams for the future.

Do something today that you love to do!

Tell a joke to make somebody laugh.

Make something special for a friend.

Plan a fun trip outdoors with your family.

Wild Weather

Life on Motunui is fun in the sun, storms, wind or rain. Trace over the weather words and draw lines to match the weather to the picture.

a

b

c

rain

sun

wind

Now talk about what you like to do in the rain, sun and wind!

Moana, Pua and Heihei are ready for a new adventure. Colour them in with your brightest pencils.

Answers

Page 9 Spirit of the Ocean

Pages 10-11 Welcome to Motunui

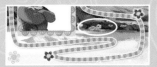

There are 10 pink flowers.

Page 15 Maui's Tattoos
a, c, d and f are real tattoos.

Page 21 Fear the Kakamora
There are 18 kakamoras so Heihei is on page 18 with his good friend, Pua.

Pages 24-25 A New Voyage

Page 26 A Sign in the Stars

1. Journey far across the waves.
2. Find Maui and his magical hook.
3. Look for a boat to set sail in.

Page 27 Nature's Treasures
a – 4, b – 6, c – 10, d – 7
1 – c, 2 – a.

Pages 36-37 Ocean Fun

Page 39 Secret Shapeshifters

Page 40 Memories
1. day
2. turtle
3. Gramma Tala is sitting down
4. Moana
5. 5 shells

Page 41 Best Friends
2 and 5 are matching pairs.

Page 50 Under the Waves
1.
2 – b, 3 – b, 4 – d.

Page 52 Musical Puzzle

Page 53 Wayfinders

Pages 54-55 Quiz Quest
1 – a, 2 – b, 3 – a, 4 – b, 5 – a,
6 – c, 7 – a, 8 – c, 9 – b.

Page 56 Moana's Message
FIND YOUR OWN WAY

Page 57 Beach Clean-up
8 coconuts, 4 baskets,
5 sticks, 2 oars.

Page 62 Something's Changed

Page 67 Wild Weather
rain – b, sun – c, wind – a.